Rabbit
Cooks up a Cunning Plan!

Andrew Fusek Peters

illustrated by

Bruno Robert

Child's Play (International) Ltd
Ashworth Rd, Bridgemead, Swindon, SN5 7YD UK
Swindon   Auburn ME   Sydney

Text © 2007 Andrew Fusek Peters   Illustrations © 2007 Child's Play (International) Ltd
Printed in Heshan, China

ISBN 978-1-84643-584-3   L240216CPL04165843

5 7 9 10 8 6 4

www.childs-play.com

Mountain Lion was one of the hungriest
and proudest animals around.
All the other animals were sick and tired
of being chased and hunted down.

One day, they all sat down and had a meeting. Opossum said, "We have to do something about that old lion!"

"My family is scared to go down to the waterhole!"

Deer agreed. "Not only that,
but I can't let my children
out of my sight without worrying!"

Bobcat added, "When my cousins hear a twig break,
they nearly die with fright. It's not good for our nerves!"

Skunk moaned, "This whole thing stinks worse than me!"

Finally, Rabbit spoke. "My family spend all their time quivering and shivering underground. This can't go on!" The other animals nodded in agreement.

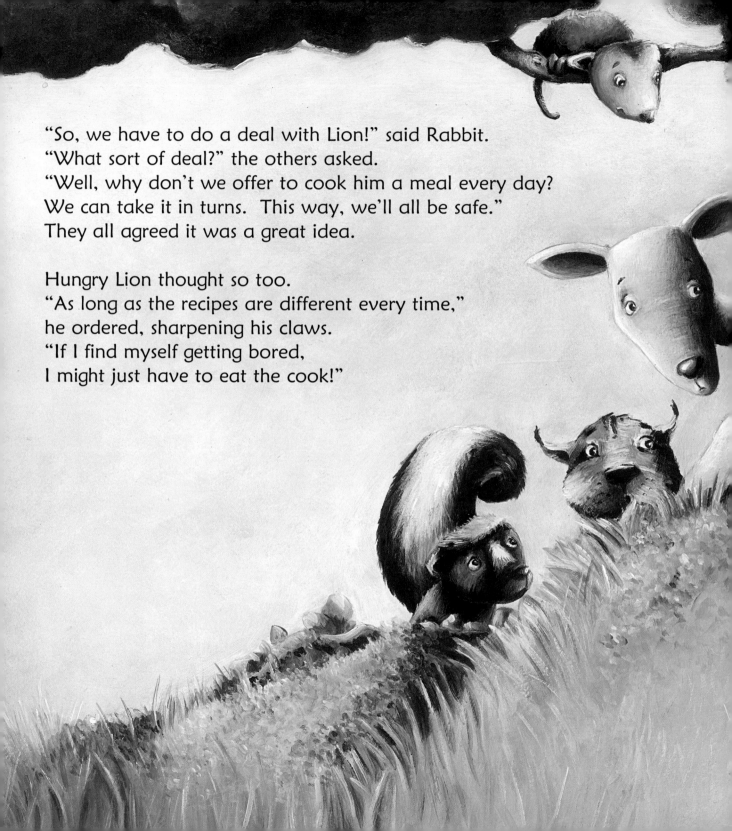

"So, we have to do a deal with Lion!" said Rabbit.
"What sort of deal?" the others asked.
"Well, why don't we offer to cook him a meal every day?
We can take it in turns. This way, we'll all be safe."
They all agreed it was a great idea.

Hungry Lion thought so too.
"As long as the recipes are different every time,"
he ordered, sharpening his claws.
"If I find myself getting bored,
I might just have to eat the cook!"

That very evening, after studying a book and cooking for hours, Opossum brought the first meal. He was trembling all over. The lion told him to stay, while he polished off the food.

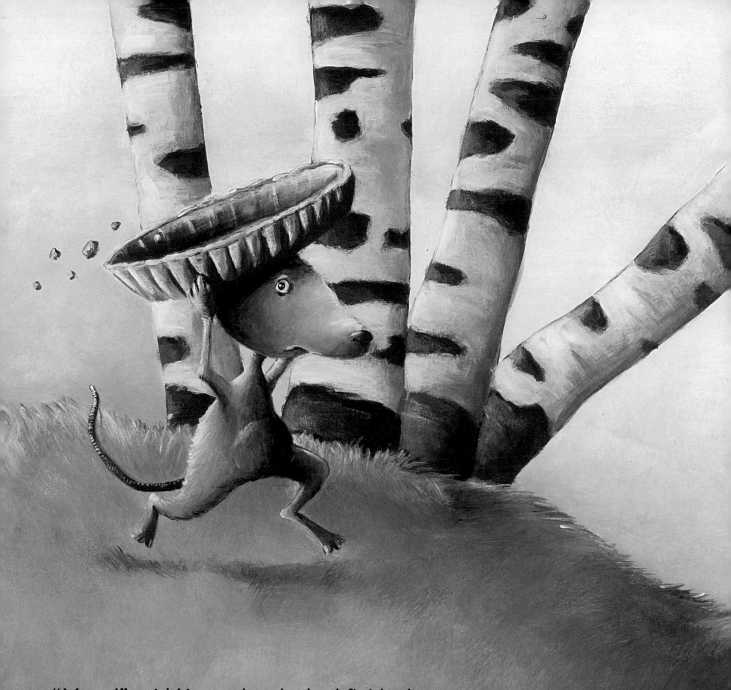

"Mmm!" said Lion, when he had finished.
"That was the best pie I've ever eaten. I reckon that will do!
Pity, though. You'd make a very nice opossum pudding!"
Opossum ran off into the woods, glad that his life had been spared.

It was the same
the following days.

Deer did a delightful
display of desserts.

Bobcat brought a beautiful bolognaise.

Skunk made a cracking curry
that smelled, well, unlike a skunk.

Lion ate like a king.
In fact, he was a king, so why not?

The next day was Rabbit's turn.

But the sun shone down
in the woods, and Rabbit
wanted to play with his friends.

After a few hours
of Catch and Hide-and-Seek,
he realized it was getting late
and he hadn't even started cooking.
Rabbit was in a pickle. What could he do?

An idea ran through his mind.
Yes...why not? Rabbit found
a patch of mud, and rolled
right around until
he was a mess.

He picked up a stone,
and made a scratch on his face.
Then he limped all the way
to see Mountain Lion.
"Rabbit!" snarled Lion.
"You're late and I'm hungry!"

Rabbit forced a tear out of his eye.
"Oh Lion, I had made the most magnificent
meat marinade, when it was stolen!"

"Stolen, eh?"
hissed the lion,
"And who by?"
"Well, sir. It was
another lion. Only
this beast was bigger
and badder than you!!!
That's why I'm in
such a state."

Lion reared up on his haunches.
His ears went red and his eyes were on fire.

Rabbit stretched out his story,
until he almost believed it himself.

"His claws are sharper,
his fangs are longer,
his roar is louder.
I'd better not lead you to him
or he might beat you!"

Lion had heard enough.
"No-one is bigger and badder than me!
Show me this imposter, Rabbit, and I might spare your life!"
Rabbit turned tail and scampered off through the woods.
Lion leapt after him, grumbling and rumbling with anger.

At last, they came to a well
in the middle of a clearing.

Rabbit trembled all over. "He...li...li...lives in a lair, down there!"
"Does he indeed?" growled the lion. "We'll see about that!"
Lion leapt up onto the edge of the well
and peered down into the darkness.
"Who stole my food?" he snarled.

An echo snarled back
MY food...MY food!"
The sun broke out
from behind the clouds
and shone down
into the well.

Lion immediately saw his enemy!
"Who do you think you are?" he roared.
The echo had an answer for that. *"Who do you think YOU are?*
Who do you think YOU are? Who do you think YOU are?"
Lion roared and his enemy roared back.

It was too much. Lion bared his fangs and leapt
into the darkness, as his enemy jumped towards him.
It was a long, long drop down to the bottom of the well,
followed by a big splash. That was the end of the lion,
who truly was his own worst enemy.

Which goes to show that it's brains and not brawn
that always wins the day, as Rabbit danced all the way home.

Deer, Opossum, Skunk and Bobcat
cooked up a feast for their hero
and declared Rabbit to be the cleverest
and wisest of all the animals!